The Adventures of MOUSE DEER

FAVORITE TALES OF SOUTHEAST ASIA

Told by Aaron Shepard
Pictures by Kim Gamble

Skyhook Press
Friday Harbor, Washington

For Taty, Vinia, and Rani

12TH ANNIVERSARY EDITION

Text and music © 1997, 2005, 2017 by Aaron Shepard
Pictures copyright © 1997, 2005, 2017 by Kim Gamble

Author portrait by Toni Goffe and Angelo Lopez

"Mouse Deer and Tiger" first appeared in Australia's *School Magazine,* April 1997. "Mouse Deer and Crocodile" first appeared in *School Magazine,* March 1997, and in *Spider,* June 2001. "Mouse Deer and Farmer" first appeared in *School Magazine,* May 1997.

Library of Congress subject headings:
Folklore—Indonesia
Folklore—Malaysia

Ages 4–9

Version 3.0

Contents

Mouse Deer's Song

Words and Music by Aaron Shepard

I'm quick and smart as I can be. Try and try, but you can't catch me!

About the Stories

You know about Brer Rabbit from the southern United States. You may also know about Anansi the Spider from West Africa. These animals are called "tricksters," because they trick other animals in the stories. There are many trickster animals around the world, and stories told about one are often told about others.

Mouse Deer is the favorite trickster of Indonesia and Malaysia, two countries of Southeast Asia. But what is a mouse deer? It is an animal about the size of a cat, and it lives in the jungles of Africa, Asia, and many Pacific islands. It has the legs and the tail of a deer, and the face and the body of a mouse—but it is not really a mouse or a deer.

The mouse deer eats only plants, but lots of animals eat the mouse deer. To stay alive, it must be quick and smart. That is why the Indonesians and Malaysians have made Mouse Deer their favorite trickster. Any of their boys or girls can tell you tales about him.

Here are some of those tales.

1

Mouse Deer
and
Tiger

"I'm quick and smart as I can be.
Try and try, but you can't catch me!"

Mouse Deer sang his song as he walked through the forest. He was looking for tasty fruits and roots and shoots.

Though he was small, he was not afraid. He knew that many big animals wanted to eat him. But first they had to catch him!

Then he heard something. *Rowr!*

There was Tiger!

"Hello, Mouse Deer. I was just getting hungry. Now you can be my lunch."

Mouse Deer didn't want to be lunch. He looked around and thought fast. He saw a mud puddle.

"I'm sorry, Tiger. I can't be your lunch. The King has ordered me to guard his pudding."

"His pudding?" said Tiger.

"Yes. There it is." Mouse Deer pointed to the mud puddle. "It has the best taste in the world. The King doesn't want anyone else to eat it."

Tiger looked longingly at the puddle. "I would like to taste the King's pudding."

"Oh, no, Tiger! The King would be very angry."

"Just one little taste, Mouse Deer! The King will never know."

"Well, all right, Tiger. But first let me run far away, so no one will blame me."

"All right, Mouse Deer, you can go now."

Mouse Deer ran quickly out of sight.

"Imagine!" said Tiger. "The King's pudding!" He took a big mouthful.

Phooey! He spit it out.

"Yuck! Ugh! Bleck! That's no pudding. That's mud!"

Tiger ran through the forest. *Rowr!* He caught up with Mouse Deer.

"Mouse Deer, you tricked me once. But now you will be my lunch!"

Mouse Deer looked around and thought fast. He saw a wasp nest in a tree.

"I'm sorry, Tiger. I can't be your lunch. The King has ordered me to guard his drum."

"His drum?" said Tiger.

"Yes. There it is." Mouse Deer pointed to the wasp nest. "It has the best sound in the

world. The King doesn't want anyone else to hit it."

Tiger said, "I would like to hit the King's drum."

"Oh, no, Tiger! The King would be very angry."

"Just one little hit, Mouse Deer! The King will never know."

"Well, all right, Tiger. But first let me run far away, so no one will blame me."

"All right, Mouse Deer, you can go now."

Mouse Deer ran quickly out of sight.

"Imagine!" said Tiger. "The King's drum!" He reached up and hit it. *Pow*.

Bzzzzzzzzzzzz. The wasps all flew out. They started to sting Tiger.

"Ouch! Ooch! Eech! That's no drum. That's a wasp nest!"

Tiger ran away. But the wasps only followed him! *Bzzzzzzzzzzzz.*

"Ouch! Ooch! Eech!"

Tiger came to a stream. He jumped in—*splash!*—and stayed underwater as long as he could. At last the wasps went away.

Then Tiger jumped out. *Rowr!* He ran through the forest till he found Mouse Deer.

"Mouse Deer, you tricked me once. You tricked me twice. But now you will be my lunch!"

Mouse Deer looked around and thought fast. He saw a cobra! The giant snake was coiled asleep on the ground.

"I'm sorry, Tiger. I can't be your lunch. The King has ordered me to guard his belt."

"His belt?" said Tiger.

"Yes. There it is." Mouse Deer pointed to the cobra. "It's the best belt in the world. The King doesn't want anyone else to wear it."

Tiger said, "I would like to wear the King's belt."

"Oh, no Tiger! The King would be very angry."

"Just for one moment, Mouse Deer! The King will never know."

"Well, all right, Tiger. But first let me run far away, so no one will blame me."

"All right, Mouse Deer, you can go now."

Mouse Deer ran quickly out of sight.

"Imagine!" said Tiger. "The King's belt!" He started to wrap it around himself.

The cobra woke up. *Sssssssssssss*. It didn't wait for Tiger to finish wrapping. It wrapped itself around Tiger. Then it squeezed him and bit him. *Sstt!*

"Ooh! Ow! Yow! That's no belt. That's a cobra! Help! Mouse Deer! Help!"

But Mouse Deer was far away. And as he went, he sang his song.

"I'm quick and smart as I can be.
Try and try, but you can't catch me!"

2

Mouse Deer
and
Crocodile

One day, Mouse Deer went down to the river. He wanted to take a drink. But he knew Crocodile might be waiting underwater to eat him.

Mouse Deer had an idea. He said out loud, "I wonder if the water's warm. I'll put in my leg and find out."

But Mouse Deer didn't put in his leg. Instead, he picked up a stick with his mouth and put in one end.

Chomp! Crocodile grabbed the stick and pulled it underwater.

Mouse Deer laughed. "Silly Crocodile! Don't you know a stick from a leg?"

And he ran off to drink somewhere else!

Another day, Mouse Deer went back to the river. All he saw there was a floating log. But he knew Crocodile looked like a log when he floated.

Mouse Deer had an idea. He said out loud, "If that log is really Crocodile, it won't talk. But if it's really just a log, it will tell me."

He listened. A rough voice said, "I'm really just a log."

Mouse Deer laughed. "Silly Crocodile! Do you think a log can talk?"

And off he ran again!

Another day, Mouse Deer wanted to cross the river. He wanted to eat tasty fruits and roots and shoots on the other side. But he didn't want Crocodile to eat him first!

Mouse Deer had an idea. He called out, "Crocodile!"

Crocodile rose from the water. "Hello, Mouse Deer. Have you come to be my breakfast?"

"Not today, Crocodile. I have orders from the King. He wants me to count all the crocodiles."

"The King!" said Crocodile. "Tell us what to do."

"You must line up from this side of the river to the other side."

Crocodile got all his friends and family. They lined up across the river.

Mouse Deer jumped onto Crocodile's back. "One."

He jumped onto the next crocodile. "Two."
And the next. "Three."
Mouse Deer kept jumping till he jumped off on the other side of the river.

"How many are there?" called Crocodile.

"Just enough!" said Mouse Deer. "And all silly!"

Then he went off singing his song.

**"I'm quick and smart as I can be.
Try and try, but you can't catch me!"**

3

Mouse Deer
and
Farmer

Mouse Deer loved to eat the fruits and roots and shoots of the forest. But he loved something else even more.

He loved the vegetables in Farmer's garden.

One day, Mouse Deer went to the edge of the forest. He looked out at row after row of vegetables.

"Mmmm," said Mouse Deer. "Juicy cucumbers! Yummy yams!" He started into the garden.

Snap! "Oh!"

His leg was caught in a snare! Mouse Deer pulled and pulled. But he could not get away.

"Oh, no!" he said. "Farmer will have me for dinner!"

Then he saw Farmer coming. Mouse Deer thought fast. He lay on the ground and made his body stiff.

"Well, well," said Farmer. "Look what I caught. A mouse deer! But he looks dead."

Farmer pushed him with his foot. Mouse Deer didn't move.

"Maybe he's been dead a long time," said Farmer. "Too bad! I guess we can't eat him."

He pulled Mouse Deer's leg out of the snare. Then he tossed Mouse Deer back into the forest.

Mouse Deer landed with a soft *plop*. Then he jumped up and ran. Behind him, he heard Farmer yell.

"Hey! You tricked me!"

Mouse Deer laughed. "Farmer is smart. But Mouse Deer is smarter!"

A few days passed. Mouse Deer kept thinking about all those vegetables. One day, he went back to the edge of the forest.

"Mmmm," said Mouse Deer. "Tasty gourds! Scrumptious sweet potatoes!"

Then he saw something new. It looked like a man. But its head was a coconut, and its body was rubber.

"A scarecrow!" said Mouse Deer. "That silly Farmer. Does he think he can scare me with that? I'll show him how scared I am!"

Mouse Deer marched up to the scarecrow. "Take this!" He gave it a big kick.

But his leg stuck to the scarecrow. The scarecrow was covered with sticky sap from a rubber tree!

"Let me go!" said Mouse Deer. He pulled and he pulled. Then he pushed with his other front leg.

That leg stuck too.

"Turn me loose!" He pulled and he pulled. Then he pushed with his two back legs.

They stuck too.

"PUT ME DOWN!" He pulled and he pushed and he pulled and he pushed. But Mouse Deer was trapped.

Then he saw Farmer. Mouse Deer thought fast. But he didn't have any ideas!

"Well, well," said Farmer. "How nice of you to come back."

He pulled Mouse Deer off the scarecrow and carried him to the house. He put him outside in an empty chicken coop.

"I'll keep you here tonight," said Farmer. "And tomorrow you'll be our dinner."

All that night, Mouse Deer couldn't sleep. He didn't want to be dinner! When the sun rose, Mouse Deer just lay there sadly.

Then he heard something. "Why, it's Mouse Deer! So Farmer caught you at last. It serves you right!"

It was Farmer's dog. Mouse Deer thought fast.

"What do you mean, Dog? Farmer didn't catch me."

"Then why are you in the coop?" said Dog.

"Because there aren't enough beds in the

house. You see, Farmer is holding a feast tomorrow. And I'm the guest of honor."

"Guest of honor?" said Dog. "That's not fair! I've been his loyal friend for years, and you're just a thief. The guest of honor should be me!"

"You know, Dog, you're right. Why don't you take my place? When Farmer sees you in here, he'll make you the guest of honor instead."

"Really?" said Dog. "You don't mind?"

"Not at all," said Mouse Deer. "You deserve it."

"Mouse Deer, you're not so bad after all. Thank you!" Dog lifted the latch and opened the door.

"You're welcome, Dog. Enjoy the feast."

Mouse Deer ran for the forest. Then he watched from the forest edge. He saw Farmer come out and stare at Dog. Then he heard Farmer yell.

"You stupid dog! You let the mouse deer get away!"

Mouse Deer laughed. "Farmer will have to find a different dinner now!" Then he went off singing his song.

"I'm quick and smart as I can be.
Try and try, but you can't catch me!"

Author Online!

On Aaron Shepard's Web site, you can

- Learn more about Mouse Deer and his stories.
- Hear the tune from Mouse Deer's song.
- Find a script for reader's theater, to act out these stories with friends and classmates.
- Download color posters of the story characters.
- Find many more stories, scripts, and other treats.
- Sign up for Aaron's email bulletin.

www.aaronshep.com

CPSIA information can be obtained
at www.ICGtesting.com
Printed in the USA
BVOW05s1229291117
500835BV00042B/154/P

9 781620 355251